D0382698

PIKES PEAK LIBRARY DISTRICT
16025434 8

mama

Eleanor Schick

Marshall Cavendish

NEW YORK

Marshall Cavendish
99 White Plains Road
Tarrytown, NY 10591
The text of this book is set in 18 point Adobe Caslon .
The illustrations are rendered in watercolor.
Printed in Hong Kong
First edition
1 3 5 6 4 2

Library of Congress Cataloging-in-Publication Data
Mama / by Eleanor Schick.
p. cm.
Summary: A child remembers special moments with Mama and starts to feel better after grieving over her death.
ISBN 0-7614-5060-2
[1. Grief Fiction. 2. Death Fiction. 3. Mother and child Fiction.] I. Title.
PZ7.S3445Mam 2000 [E]—dc21 99-16373 CIP

For Anne and Louise

Mama, you've been gone for a long time.

I still miss you. Louise says it's important to remember how it was when you were here.

I remember the night you told me you were sick. You said you might not get well. But you said you would try. That was the night we waited for the moon. We sat on your bed. I could feel the cool, summer wind in my hair. I looked for the moon, but all I could see was the dark of the buildings getting darker, and the blue of the sky getting deeper blue. "Keep watching," you told me. A light went on in one window, then another. Then another. That's all I saw. "Keep watching," you told me.

You pointed to a tiny arc of white behind a chimney. "Keep watching that," you whispered. I did. And it grew bigger, and bigger, until it was whole and round and separate, rising very slowly in the sky. We watched it for a long time. I leaned into your arms. I could feel you breathing. I closed my eyes and listened to the song you sang to me, until I fell asleep.

I remember the last day you could take me to the park. It was fall, and the leaves were turning. We pointed to the trees, naming their colors: orange, red, yellow, rust, and all the different greens. We walked along the lanes. I climbed the highest rocks, pretending they were mountains, while you watched.

We went to the playground where you pushed me on the swing. I went higher and higher, till I could see the buildings, beyond the trees, on the other side of town. You said, “Soon you’ll be pumping all by yourself and you won’t even need me.” I’ll always need you, I thought to myself. I couldn’t imagine ever not needing you.

I remember the first day Louise came to help you make dinner. She came every day after that, and stayed later and later. She was standing at the sink, washing vegetables. You were peeling potatoes, putting them in a big, yellow bowl. Louise was singing. It was a song about God. I remember how you closed your eyes and hummed. Then your words joined hers, and the song was like a prayer, filling the room. The sunlight on the wall was turning golden. I remembered how I felt when I watched the moon rising. I could see it in my mind. As you and Louise sang, I drew the moon.

All that feels far away now, like a dream. Everything changed that winter morning when they took you away—to the hospital. You were so sick, you couldn't even tell me goodbye. When I came home from school, Papa was there instead of you. He was sad, and far away. So far away, I couldn't find him. That's when he told me you died. I felt like I was spinning off the edge of the world. I cried and cried and cried. That's the time Louise came in the afternoon. That's when she came to stay. She said, "Sometimes life just hurts too much, and all we can do is cry." Louise held me, and rocked me in her arms. She said, "It's going to be alright, child." And I cried even more.

Time passed. Papa worked all the time, and when he didn't, he was quiet, and far away. Louise just did her chores, and let me stay near her if I wanted to. I wanted to. She'd say, "It's going to be alright, child," but I didn't think so. One day I told her, "If Mama really loved me, she wouldn't have left." Louise took me in her big arms. She said, "I know your mama never stopped loving you. And she didn't leave you, child. She's with you still." She put her hand over my heart. "She's right here, inside of you," Louise said. "She always will be."

The full moon came up that night. I watched it rise, filling the night, and my room, with light. I could feel you near me. I could feel you telling me, "It's going to be alright." I could feel myself believing that it would be.

Louise takes me to the park, now, with Amy. We climb up on the highest rocks, pretending they're mountains. We run through the leaves. We fall down in them, throwing them in the air and laughing. We go to the playground. We swing on swings. I can pump all by myself now. I go high enough to see the buildings, beyond the trees, on the other side of town.

Still, there are times when I miss you. Like when the leaves have all fallen off the trees, and the branches are dark and bare—or when the afternoon light is just one certain color, and I can smell winter coming—or when night comes early, and the cold creeps through my window panes, and I can see my breath on the glass—I feel an old sadness I can't name. In those times, Louise just holds me. She says, "It's going to be alright, child," and I know it will be.

Now, when Louise is putting dinner up to cook and I'm helping her, and she's singing, and I sing with her—I feel you with me.

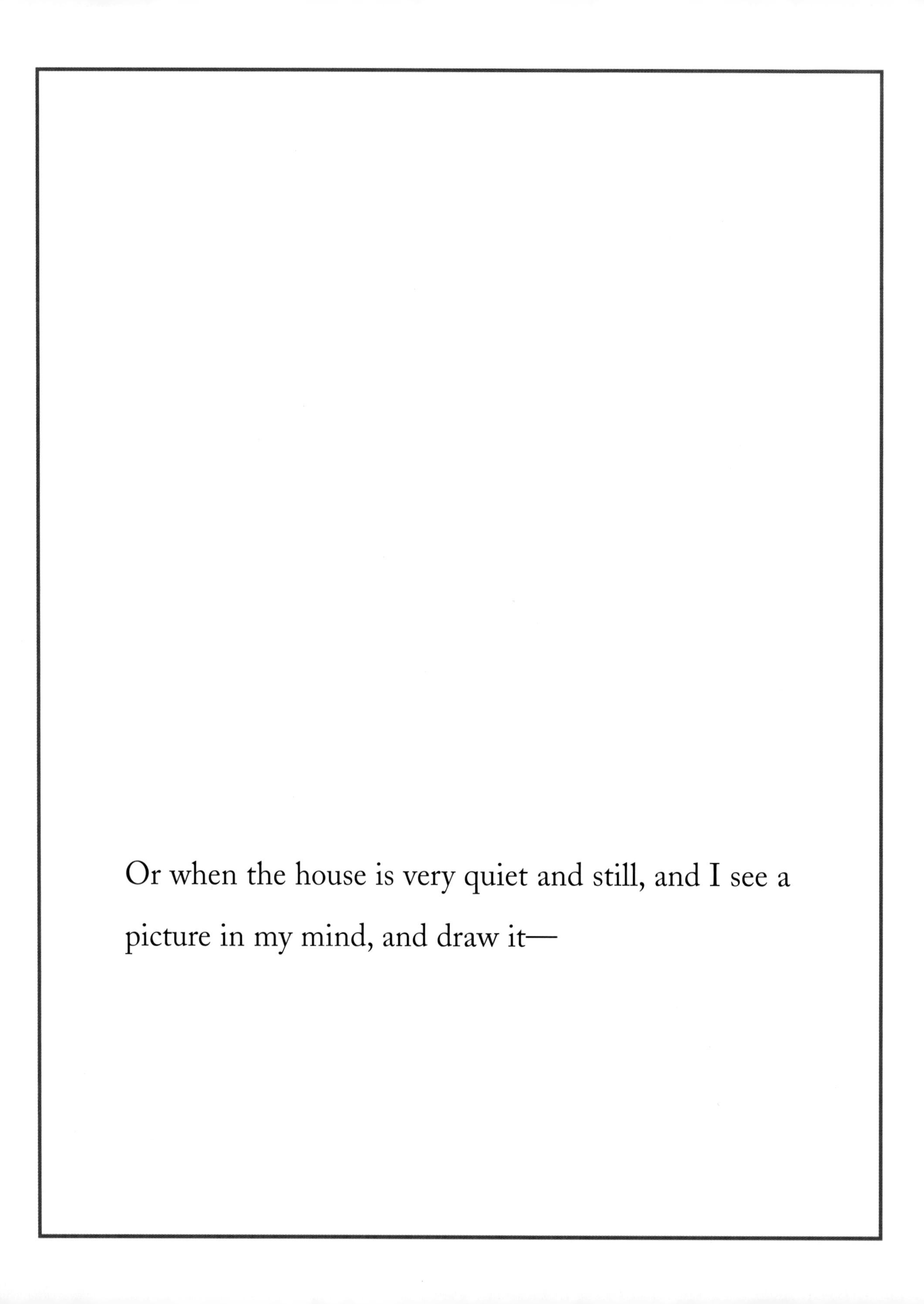

Or when the house is very quiet and still, and I see a picture in my mind, and draw it—

or when I see the moon—

I know you're with me. All the time, in everything.

You're in my heart, Mama. You always will be.